TABLE OF CONTENTS

SCENT evidence K9 ®
BRINGING THE LOST HOME

Rex the Rescue Pup

Written by
Cassie Coley

Illustrated by
Joe Blanton

Photography by
Tammy Grider

Edited by
Donna Coley

Dedicated to Rex Stockham
Father, Husband, Friend and Dedicated to
Bringing the Lost Home

ISBN 13: 978-1985123922

Scent Evidence K9
2813 Industrial Plaza Drive
Tallahassee, FL 32301

www.scentevidencek9.com

Chapter 1

A PUP'S PLACE

This is Rex; an eager, kind, playful, and stubborn bloodhound pup.

Rex has big floppy brown ears with black spots, droopy eyes, and long skinny legs. Rex is only one year old and hasn't quite grown into his large paws, so he is a little clumsy.

He lives on a big farm filled with all different kinds of animals and creatures.

He shares his home with chickens, sheep, horses, goats, cows, and even a few cats -

along with many other types of dogs!

Every animal has a job that helps the farm run smoothly and keeps everyone cared for and safe.

Rex recently turned one, which means he is now old enough to find his role on the farm. He is very excited to start a job.

Rex has watched the other dogs on the farm perform their roles day in and day out, exciting jobs like retrieving, guarding, and herding sheep. Rex wanted to try them all!

Chapter 2

THE SEARCH BEGINS

Rex decided he would start his search by visiting Lucy, the golden retriever. Lucy has amazing talent, and Rex enjoys her kind, mothering nature.

He found her practicing with a human child who lived on the farm. Rex ran to them just as the little boy looked down to Lucy and asked her,

"Are you ready girl?"
Lucy looked up to him with a focused gaze and nodded.

The boy pulled back his arm, preparing to throw the tennis ball in the air. Before it left his hand, Lucy was off. Rex watched and couldn't help but be amazed. She flashed by him like a streak of gold lightening.

She easily beat the ball to its destination, scooped it up in her mouth with a simple swoop of her nose, and trotted back to them with her head held high.

The boy threw the ball a few more times, and each time Lucy retrieved it quickly and delivered it perfectly, even without slobber!

Finally, after a very impressive retrieval that required Lucy to jump a few feet in the air, she dropped the ball at the boy's feet and lay down panting.

Lucy looked around and saw Rex, "Well hi there, little pup. Would you like to give retrieving a try? I sure could use a break."

"You betcha!" Rex barked loudly with a little jump in the air. Lucy giggled at his eager response and nudged the ball towards him with her nose. The child looked at Rex with a grin and picked up the ball to give it a toss.

Rex was off.

He leapt after the ball with all the energy inside him!

For a moment, he felt like a flash of lightening himself... until he tripped over his long ears and went tumbling down the green hill.

Rex finally stopped rolling when he reached the fence. He shook his head and looked around. The ball was nowhere to be seen. He turned around and saw Lucy running toward him with the ball in her mouth.

When she reached him, she set the ball down and exclaimed, "Are you okay little guy?"

"I think so," Rex replied with another shake of his head.

"Looks like those long ears and legs of yours got in the way, huh?"
Lucy giggled affectionately.

"Maybe retrieving isn't the best job for you. Better keep sniffing
around. There are plenty of safer things for you to do
here on the farm," she offered.

Disappointed and still a little dizzy, Rex thanked Lucy
for letting him join her and set off searching for another job.

Chapter 3

AN ADVENTURE WITH OTTO

Rex decided to visit Otto the German shepherd. Otto is a guard dog and protects the entire farm. Rex saw Otto patrolling the edge of the property near the white fence. He trotted up to Otto, excited but a little nervous about talking to such an important dog.

"Uh, hi there Otto," Rex started, "I was wondering if maybe I could ask you a favor." "Make it quick," Otto replied shortly.

"Of course," said Rex with a sure shake of his head. "Well, I'd like to see if guarding the farm might be something I could do.

Would it be alright if I came along with you for a bit, and helped you with your morning checkpoints?"

"I see no problem with that," said Otto, turning his head from the fence towards Rex. "If you can stay focused and keep up with the pace." Otto shouted back to Rex as he ran ahead to continue patrolling along the fence. "I'm sure I can!" barked Rex as he pranced proudly up to meet him.

"Good. Here's what you need to know: you have to keep your eyes open and be able to know a threat when you see one. Think you can do that?" Otto asked.

"Oh, definitely!" Rex barked confidently. But Otto was already too busy to respond.

They had reached the chicken coop on the south side of the farm and Otto was now lurking quietly between the fence and the back wall of the coop.

With a sudden jerk, he began pawing at the ground and barking viciously.

Rex saw something black slither away into the grassy field beyond the farm.

He gasped, it was a snake trying to get the chicken eggs!

Otto turned back to Rex. "See? You have to be quick and ready for anything." he said with a serious look.

"Wow!" Rex whispered to himself. "This is serious!"

They patrolled the farm a little while longer. Rex kept his nose to the ground, determined to sniff out a threat. Until suddenly he caught a whiff of something he'd never smelled before, something foul, and offensive to his nose.

"It must be something dangerous." Rex thought to himself. He followed the scent to the back edge of the property with Otto directly behind him, continuing to address his checkpoints but keeping aware of Rex's direction.

They came to a dip in the fence surrounded by mud. Rex heard an unusual sound coming from the other side of the mud pile, a chorus of strange moans.

"This must be something scary!" Rex thought as his heart began to pound uncontrollably. He leapt on top of the mud pile, barking loudly and pawing at the creatures on the other side. When he was close enough to see what the creatures were, he saw a dozen four-legged, little, green, rubbery looking things.

He then heard Otto laughing loudly behind him. Rex stopped barking,
looked at Otto, and tilted his head in confusion.
Otto was barely able to get his words out through the waves of laughter.

"Those...are... HAHAHAH... they're bullfrogs... Hehehehehe...
just little toads...
Not exactly.... Oh man hahahaha... they aren't dangerous...
hahaha... just stinky. "

Rex's cheeks flushed red as he walked off the mudpile back
under the fence beside Otto.

"Oh" Rex said quietly as he hung his head.

"That nose of yours would certainly get you in trouble patrolling."
Otto said with a chuckle.

Seeing the look of discouragement on Rex's face, he added, "But don't
be discouraged little guy. There are plenty of other jobs on the
farm I'm sure would suit you."

Frustrated, Rex thought to himself, "I've blown it twice today
and it's not even afternoon yet."

Was there anything left to do on the farm?

Chapter 4

ONE LAST SHOT

He heard a group of dogs barking wildly, and remembered,
"Yes there is, sheep herding! I still haven't tried herding sheep!"

Rex saw the three herd dogs rallying the sheep into
the west pasture. He ran eagerly over to them.

"Hi there Colleen! Billy! Tilly!" Rex said, excitedly.

The three dogs turned and all barked in unison, "Hi Rex!"
Colleen, a collie who was the leader of the sheepherders, added,
"Give us just a moment to finish getting these cotton balls into
the pasture and we'll be right with you."

"No rush." Rex barked back.

He watched as Bill and Tilly, Colleen's helpers, ran tireless circles around the sheep, making sure all filed into the pasture.

Rex couldn't help but laugh at the sight of Billy and Tilly. They had tiny legs and were much smaller than any of the other dogs on the farm, but they sure could move. They looked like they were swimming in the pasture, working to keep their heads above the stalks of grass, but their serious and determined faces proved that they experienced no feelings of inferiority.

Once the sheep were in the pasture, Colleen made her way toward Rex, and Bill and Tilly quickly followed behind her.

Well, top of the morning to you lad." she exclaimed with a bright expression. "Top of the morning!" Billy and Tilly echoed behind her.

"Uh, good morning," replied Rex.

"What can we sheep herders do for you this fine day, little bloodhound pup?" asked Colleen.

"Well," started Rex, "I'm trying to figure out what role on the farm I would best fit, and I wanted to try my paw at sheepherding. Could I tag along with you for a bit?"

"Why of course!" Colleen exclaimed, "We could always use another set of paws and a loud barker to wrangle these cotton balls." Behind her Bill and Tilly nodded their heads in agreement with great exaggeration.

"Come along lad; We are off to move the herd on the east side of the farm to the pasture on the west side. I'll explain how it all works on the way."

Rex trotted alongside Colleen, while Billy and Tilly sang a working song behind them. Rex smiled at the lighthearted spirit of the team.

"Alright," Colleen said in a matter of fact tone, "All you really need to know is to bark and move quickly. Barking motivates the cotton balls to move in the direction we want them to go. And if we're quick enough we can keep stragglers from falling behind the group. It's all about moving as one... and being as loud as you can!"

"HEAR! HEAR!" barked Billy and Tilly at the top of their lungs, partly to end their song, but also to drive home Colleen's point.

"Seems easy enough." Rex thought to himself.

"Alright, I guess I'm ready to give it a try." Rex said quietly, trying not to get his hopes up after his last two failures.

"Well no reason to be so sheepish lad." Colleen responded with a playful look on her face.

"So sheepish! What a good one that is!" Billy and Tilly exclaimed while they rolled around on the ground laughing hysterically.

Rex grinned and relaxed a bit.

"Alright, here we are," Colleen said as they came up to meet the sheep grazing in the east pasture.

"Ready all?" she questioned with a half grin.
"Ready ma'am," replied Billy and Tilly.
"Oh yes! Me too!" added Rex.

"Let's go!" Colleen announced with a bark.

They all broke out into sprints rounding up the sheep.
Rex started toward the last side of the herd and began barking
loudly which sounded more like a howl or a song.

The sheep all looked at him with confusion at first,
but the confusion quickly turned to amusement.

"What's he doing?" one sheep said to the other.

"I think he's crying." a smaller sheep shouted out.

"No, no, he's singing, right?" interjected another sheep closer to Rex.

"No, no, he must be speaking a different language. I've never
heard the likes of it," cackled an older female
on the outskirt of the herd.

An older male sheep standing next to her turned and commented,
"Well whatever it is, it's the funniest thing I've heard."

The sheep all stopped in their tracks and continued laughing hysterically at
Rex's bark. They stopped paying attention to the other herd dogs altogether.

Colleen, Billy, and Tilly, ran around the herd a few more times, barking
with great focus, but with no success.
They finally gave up and walked over to Rex.

"Why don't we take a minute to chat Rex?" Colleen said,
"Billy, Tilly – you two look after the cotton balls."

"Not again." Rex thought as his heart sank to his paws and he
followed Colleen to the edge of the field.

"Listen lad." Colleen started.

"I know, I know." Rex interrupted,
"I don't have what it takes to herd sheep.
My bark's too funny and the sheep won't listen to me.
You don't have to tell me. I already know."

"My ears and legs are too long to retrieve, my nose is too distracting to patrol, and my bark is too funny to herd. I just don't have what it takes to work on this farm!" He huffed dramatically.

And then, to Rex's horror, he began to whimper and cry.

Colleen looked down at him, her eyes full of compassion.

"Well that's just not true. Why, I have known you since you were born.
I've seen how kind you are to all the animals and
how quick you are to offer a helping paw.

There's plenty of jobs on this farm. A smart, kind,
capable pup like yourself is sure to find something to do!"
"I've tried all day!" complained Rex, "But I've failed at everything."

Colleen sighed deeply and gave him a comforting smile,
"Dear pup, sometimes it takes longer than one day to find your place.
And who's to say you have to do a job that already exists on the farm.

Instead of looking for a job that others have, perhaps you can do
something different using your special gifts.

Wouldn't it be something if you came up with your own role,
instead of trying to fit into one that already exists."

Rex sniffed and rubbed his eyes on his paw.
"Like what?" he asked.

"I don't know," Colleen said,
"but it's something worth thinking about, isn't it?"

"I suppose." Rex sighed.

Chapter 5

SCENT ON A MISSION

All of a sudden, Billy came running up to Colleen with Tilly only a few feet behind him. "Colleen! Colleen!" he exclaimed.

"Yes, what is it Billy?" Colleen barked to him as he ran up to her, almost runninginto her. (Billy has a difficult time stopping his little legs once they are in motion.)

"It's one of the sheep! She's missing!" he yelled through sharp breaths.

"Which one?" Colleen asked frantically as she started toward the herd. Rex followed, also concerned by the troubling news. "The small one. I think her name is Shelly." he replied.

"Oh, no." Colleen whispered. "She's very young and doesn't know the boundaries of the pasture yet. Goodness, she could have left the farm."

"What do we do?" yelped Tilly. "How do we find her?" added Billy.

"We need to start looking for her immediately." Colleen ordered. She hesitated, "Someone must stay with the sheep."

Billy and Tilly immediately barked, "We will! We'll make sure nothing happens to them ma'am."

"Thank you," said Colleen, with a sigh of relief. Concern filled her face, "But now, I need to find someone to help me bring the lost sheep home."

Rex, who had been listening quietly to their conversation, piped up,
"I think I can help Ms. Colleen."

"You do, do you?" she replied questioningly.

"Well, yes. I'm pretty good with smells. I can remember them easily and
my long ears help me pick up scent on the ground,
so I make a pretty good trailing dog"

"But there are hundreds of sheep out here. Do you really think you can pick out Shelly's smell apart from the others?" Colleen asked.

"Of course." stated Rex. "Each creature has its own unique scent, unlike any other."

"Have you smelled Shelly before?" asked Colleen.

"No, but all I need is something she's touched." replied Rex.

"Here, I know just the thing." said Colleen.

She took off toward the pasture and Rex followed.

Colleen led him to a spot of grass near the farm's fence.

"This is where she was grazing today." she informed Rex.

"Perfect." he replied, as he began sniffing around the area. He was soon able to pick up a fresh, distinctive scent that he followed to the other side of the fence.

"I think I've got it." Rex barked back to Colleen. "Follow me!"

Rex took off, following his nose wherever it took him, Colleen trailing after him. It wasn't long before they'd left the farm's property.

"Oh, no." Colleen whispered under her breathe, "This is what I feared. It's dangerous for a little sheep to be out here in the wild. She could be trapped in a hole, or what if a coyote or a bear..."

Her voice trailed off and a gasp caught in her throat.

"I care deeply about every sheep" she said in a trembling voice.

"There's no time for talk like that right now!" barked Rex. "We have to keep moving."

He was getting closer; her scent was getting stronger!

But they still couldn't see any sign of Shelly.

"Are you sure you're going the right way Rex?" Colleen questioned. "It's almost dark and I haven't seen anything that resembles Shelly."

"She's close! I know it!" barked Rex. "Just give me a few more minutes." Rex was confident, despite his many failures earlier today. This time he wasn't trying to find a job, or to impress anyone. This time he wanted to save a life, and he knew he could find Shelly. His nose led him to a mud puddle and he could see something moving around inside it.

"Stay back!" Colleen shouted as she watched Rex get closer and closer to the black, moaning, curious thing in the mud.

"You have no idea what that could be!
It could be a bear for all you know!"
Colleen warned frantically.

Rex looked closer at the creature,
covered in mud and gave a sigh of relief.
"That's no bear, Colleen! It's Shelly!"

"What?" Colleen gasped in surprise.

Rex jumped into the mud and began pushing Shelly out of the puddle with his head. She tumbled out, frantically baying and crying as Colleen rushed over to calm her.

"Oh, it is Shelly!" Colleen exclaimed. "Oh my goodness! I would have never thought that was Shelly! Rex, you're a hero!"

"Oh, calm down sweetie, we'll get you home and cleaned up right away. Don't you worry little cotton ball," Colleen cooed sweetly.

She turned to Rex with tears in her eyes.

"Rex, you did it! You did what only you could do.
And it saved someone's life!
Why, if it wasn't for that nose of yours,
mixed with your stubborn spirit,
we wouldn't have made it to Shelly in time."

Rex beamed. She was right.

He had saved Shelly by doing what only he knows how to do.

"I believe you found
your job."
Colleen added
affectionately.

"You're
Rex the Rescue Pup."

Rex the Rescue Pup
Rescue Team

You are now part of Rex's Rescue Team. You have special talents just like Rex. List what they are below. You can have someone help you.

Name _____

_____   _____

_____   _____

_____   _____

BRINGING THE LOST HOME

You have a unique scent just like Shelly the sheep and you can collect and save it with a **Scent Preservation Kit®**. www.scentevidencek9.com

Made in the USA
Columbia, SC
26 January 2023

10683926R00029